CALYPSO

Cousteau

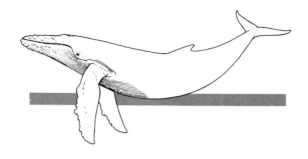

LITTLE SIMON
Simon & Schuster Building, Rockefeller Center
1230 Avenue of the Americas, New York, New York 10020

Manufactured in Singapore   10   9   8   7   6   5   4   3   2   1

CREDITS
The Cousteau Society, Jacques-Yves Cousteau, Jean-Michel Cousteau
Author: Christine Causse. Photo Editor: Judy K. Brody
Translation: Jeannine C. Morgan. Project Director: Lesley D. High. With special thanks to: Pamela Stacey.
Photographers: Chuck Davis, Flip Nicklin, Steve Arrington, Clay Wilcox, David O. Brown, Dominique Serafini.

Library of Congress Cataloging-in-Publication Data
Baleines à bosse. English, Whales / the Cousteau Society.   p.   cm.   Summary: Examines the
physical characteristics, behavior, and migration pattern of the humpback whale.
1. Whales—Juvenile literature.   [1. Humpback whale.   2. Whales.]   I. Cousteau Society.   II. Title.
QL737.C4B23813   1993   599.5—dc20   92-34176   CIP
ISBN 0-671-86564-1

The Cousteau Society

WHALES

LITTLE SIMON

Published by Simon & Schuster

New York   London   Toronto   Sydney   Tokyo   Singapore

HUMPBACK WHALES

Marine mammal

Weight and size
Baby: 1(+) tons, 13.5 feet
Adult: 30–48 tons, 42–54 feet

Life span
Approximately 50 years

Food
Krill and small fish

Reproduction
11–12 months gestation
Mates every 2–3 years, in the spring

Migrates from one region of the world to another

A protected species

This giant humpback whale is so playful, it is
sometimes called "the clown of the sea."

Its flippers are so huge, they almost look like wings.
The whale is as heavy as ten elephants!

The whale swims to the surface to breathe. It sprays out its breath, then takes another and disappears.

Diving downward into its ocean home, the whale can plunge as deep as 600 feet on a single breath.

Every year the whale journeys from icy waters to warm seas where it meets other whales.

Here they are back together again!
A group of whales is called a pod.

Together they make strange and
wonderful sounds.

This baby whale stays with its mother. She feeds the baby her milk and the baby grows quickly.

Strong and graceful like a dancer, the humpback whale playfully leaps high above the waves.

It spins and crashes down with a splash and a giant spray of foam!

Summer is coming. It is time to return to colder waters, where the humpback will find plenty of food.

The whale dives down into the sea and begins its great trip. Before too long, it will be back again.